To my sister, Adria

Clarion Books
a Houghton Mifflin Company imprint
215 Park Avenue South, New York, NY 10003
Copyright © 2006 by Jessica Meserve
First published in Great Britain in 2006 by Andersen Press Ltd.
First American edition, 2007.

The illustrations were executed in digital media.
The text was set in Blockhead Unplugged.

www.clarionbooks.com

Printed in Singapore.

Library of Congress Cataloging-in-Publication Data
Meserve, Jessica.
[Small.]
Small sister / Jessica Meserve.—1st American ed.
p. cm.
Summary: Tired of always being in Big's shadow, Small leaves home seeking freedom and happiness
but finds only loneliness, until she sees a way to prove that she can be big, too.
ISBN-13: 978-0-618-77658-0   ISBN-10: 0-618-77658-3
[1. Size—Fiction. 2. Self-actualization (Psychology)—Fiction.] I. Title.
PZ7.M5485 Sma 2007
[E]—dc22   2006014381

10 9 8 7 6 5 4 3 2 1

Small Sister

Jessica Meserve

Clarion Books • New York

Small had a **problem**.
She was stuck in Big's shadow.

Small tried to jump higher,
but Big was bouncier.

Small tried to escape,
but Big was faster.

And Big always got
the best presents.

Sometimes Big tried
to scare Small.

One day Big made
Small very angry,

13

so Small did something very mean.

Big's parrot flew away.

But when Big
found out . . .

16

. . . Small felt
even smaller.

The next day,
Small decided
to leave.

18

Nobody noticed.

Small
was free.

She tried to feel happy,

but she
was too
lonely.

High in the tree,
Small saw Big's parrot.

Low on the ground,
Small saw . . .

. . . Big.

Big was too
scared to climb
the tree.

Small
wasn't
scared.

Small felt BRAVE.

Small felt **BIG**.

Small felt very happy.

And best of all,
Small was no longer
stuck in Big's shadow.